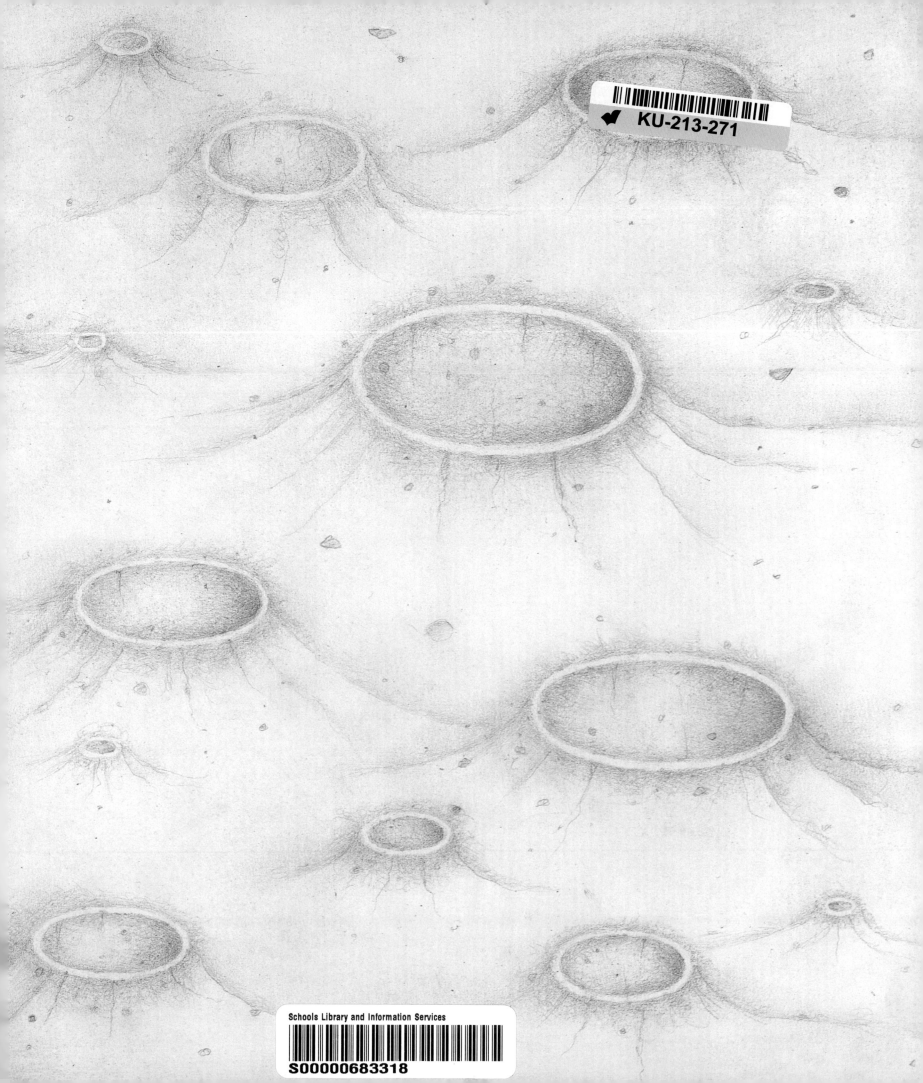

For Blue, an Earth dog - Helen

For Rosy, Phill and Benny the dog - Wayne

A TEMPLAR BOOK

First published in the UK in 2005 by Templar Publishing,
an imprint of The Templar Company plc,
Pippbrook Mill, London Road, Dorking, Surrey, RH4 1JE, UK
www.templarco.co.uk

Text copyright © 2005 by Helen Ward
Illustration copyright © 2005 by Wayne Anderson

First edition

ISBN 1-84011-864-4

Designed by Mike Jolley
Edited by A.J. Wood

Printed in China

A story by
HELEN WARD

MOON DOG

Illustrated by WAYNE ANDERSON

templar publishing

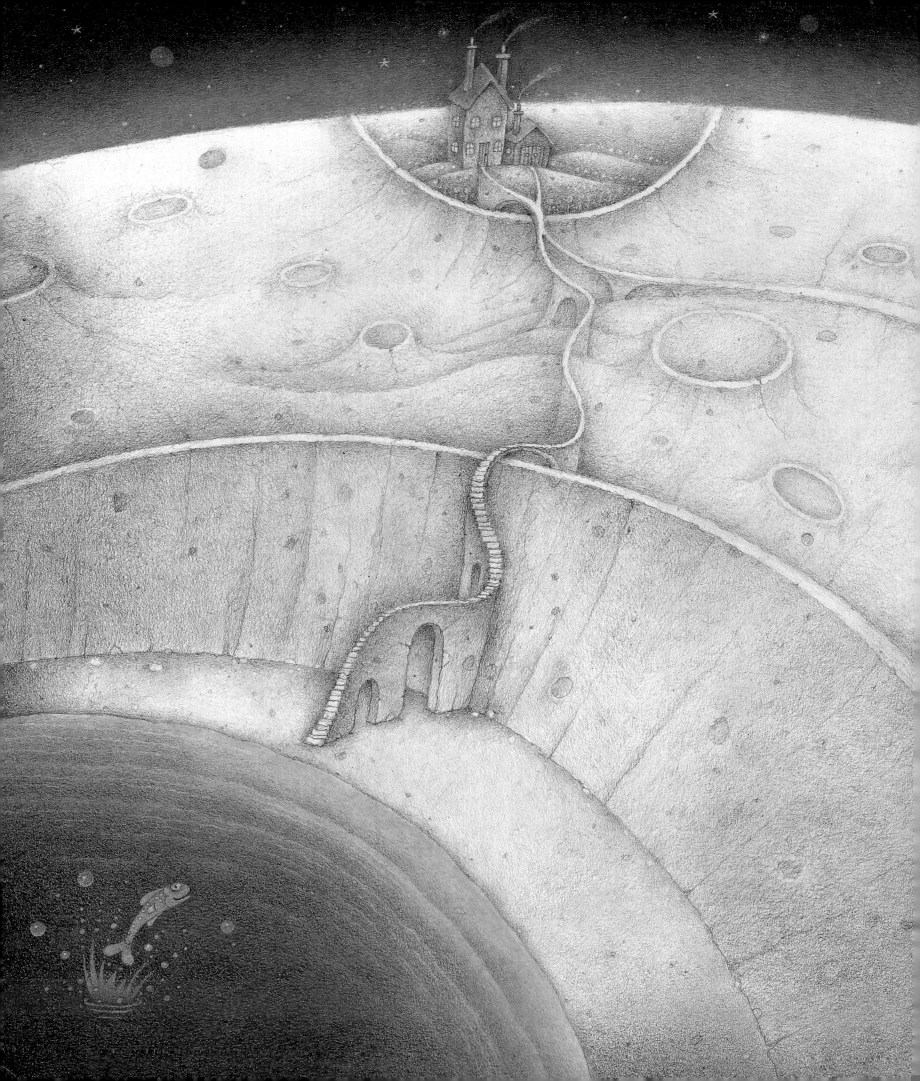

THE MOON IS USUALLY A PEACEFUL PLACE,

but once a year the gentle quietness is shattered by the arrival of...

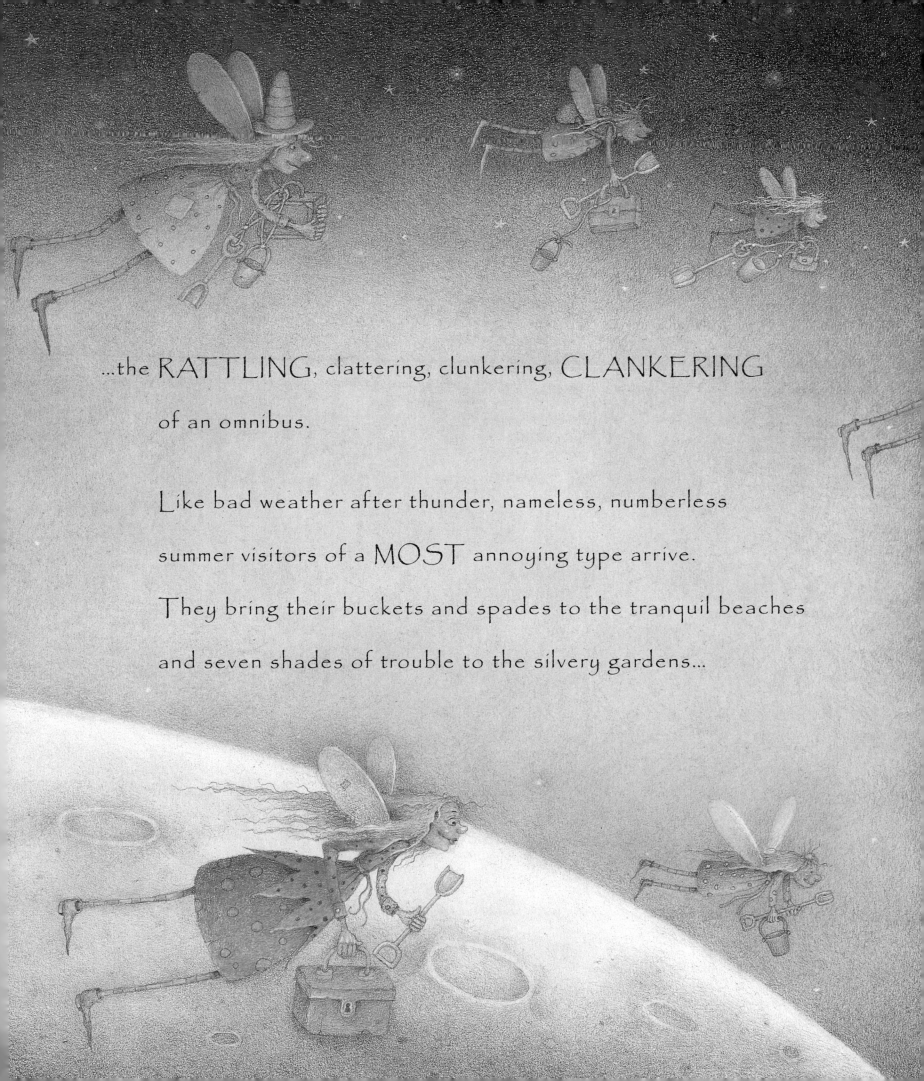

...the RATTLING, clattering, clunkering, CLANKERING

of an omnibus.

Like bad weather after thunder, nameless, numberless

summer visitors of a MOST annoying type arrive.

They bring their buckets and spades to the tranquil beaches

and seven shades of trouble to the silvery gardens...

THE MAN IN THE MOON had seen

and heard it all far, FAR TOO often before.

Each year, as soon as they arrived, he would lock and bolt

his front door, nail shut his letterbox and settle in his

comfortable armchair, with a pile of comfortable books.

With his little Moon Dog curled up happily at his feet,

the Man in the Moon would try very hard to imagine

that he was somewhere ELSE until the tiresome visitors

went home.

BUT LITTLE MOON DOG

soon tired of being cooped up indoors all day.

He loved the Man in the Moon, but he wanted

excitement and adventure. And, besides, these

strange strangers filled him with curiosity.

He watched as they poked holes in the rhumoonbarb

and unwound the runner moonbeans from their canes.

They pulled silly faces at little Moon Dog through

the window and called him out to play.

As the man in the moon

dozed in his comfortable chair, little Moon Dog

sneaked out of the back door,

and into BAD company.

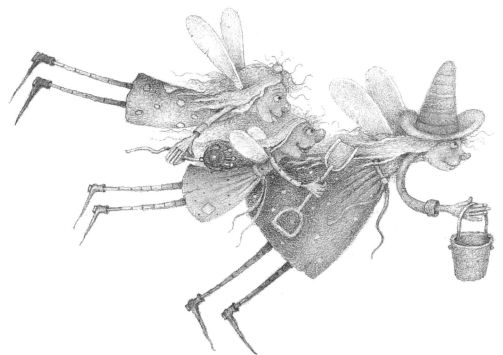

The wonderful visitors ruffled his ears and tickled him under the chin. They cuddled him and fed him honey buns and quince jelly sandwiches, with real sand, until he was as fat as a balloon.

Little Moon Dog thought his new friends were marvellous, especially when they gave him his own pair of wings. And how they LAUGHED when he bounced and flapped and tumbled after the sticks they threw for him.

THE MAN IN THE MOON called him in for his tea, but little Moon Dog was too busy playing with his CLEVER new friends to take any notice.

They taught him to pinch plums and drop them down the chimney, and to chase moonmoths across the starry sky.

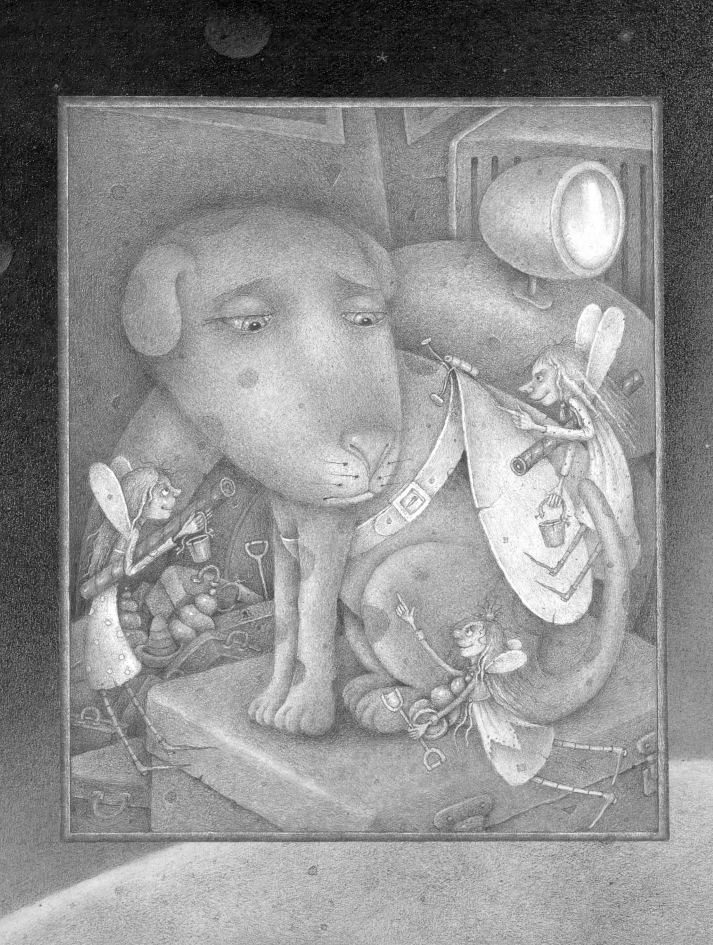

ALL TOO SOON, it was time for the visitors to leave.

Their holiday was over. Little Moon Dog sat sadly

amongst their luggage. He did not want to lose his

wonderful friends. His flappety wings flopped as they loaded

the omnibus with their luggage. So they packed him in TOO,

along with their other souvenirs, squeezed in with the sticky

moonrock and the broken buckets.

The little Moon Dog buried all thoughts of the Man in

the Moon in the back of his head. He was so in love with his

NEW friends that he wagged his tail ALL the way

back through the moonlit night.

THE MAN IN THE MOON looked on

and in every shelf and cupboard and box and basket

for little Moon Dog. He searched through the straggling

tangle of his once tidy garden. He wandered among the

sandcastles on the silvery beaches.

He called and he CALLED, but eventually the Man

in the Moon realised that his little Moon Dog...

...was FAR TOO FAR away to hear him.

IN THE SHADY WOODS of another

planet little Moon Dog had chased and had fetched

all the sticks that his bright new friends had thrown for him.

He had learned all the tricks that they could teach, and NOW

they had OTHER, better things to be doing.

They were busy muddling up the lines of summer swallows

and swapping around seeds to unsettle the spring.

Little Moon Dog wanted them to play with him, but they were too

busy making TROUBLE. They called him little Dog Stinker,

and shooed him away.

HE SAT AMONG the high branches with his wings drooping and whimpered. He watched as his friends played games with other NEW and exciting creatures.

He watched as they tricked and teased, pinched and poked,

and he realised that they weren't REALLY his friends at all.

Little Moon Dog suddenly felt very, VERY, VERY lonely.

He wished the Man in the Moon was there to comfort him.

He wished more than anything that he could

go HOME.

M EANWHILE, the Man in the Moon had tidied the silvery gardens and mended almost everything that had been broken. His little Moon Dog still had not returned. So he took down a toolbox from a high shelf, shovelled a moondust-drift away from a long-locked garage door, and turned a key in the rusty lock.

The moon grew as round as a great gold plate and a dark shadow rippled over its surface as the Man in the Moon left the peace and quiet of his home and started out on a journey. It was TIME for him to FIND his friend.

THE MAN IN THE MOON searched everywhere for his

little Moon Dog. By the time he reached the shady woods,

he was beginnning to give up hope of ever seeing him again.

But still he searched, looking low and high until one cold

evening the moon rose and cast its silvery light among the

leaves. And as it rose, a strange, sad sound echoed through

the trees; a sound that made the Man in the Moon

VERY happy indeed...

LITTLE MOON DOG'S homesick howl turned to a
wild woofing when he saw who had come to collect him.

They were SO PLEASED to see each other.

Little Moon Dog scampered and flapped about
until the Man from the Moon caught him out of the air
and hugged him and wrapped him up
in his great warm coat...

...and took him HOME.

N OW, whenever the gentle quietness of the moon is broken

by those nameless, numberless summer visitors, little

Moon Dog and his BEST and most beloved friend

go away on a holiday of their OWN.

F OR NOW the Man in the Moon AND his little Moon Dog

both agree...

...there is NOTHING quite so NASTY as a FAIRY!

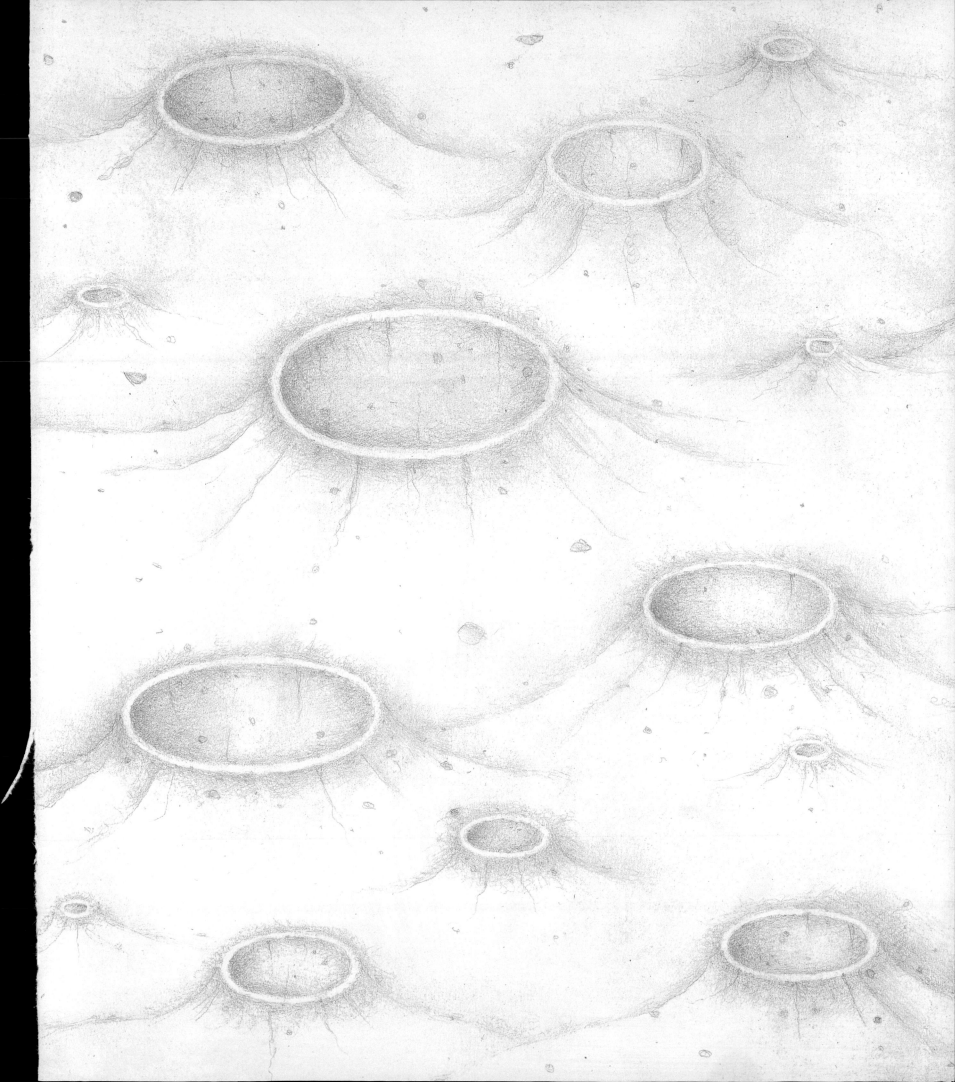

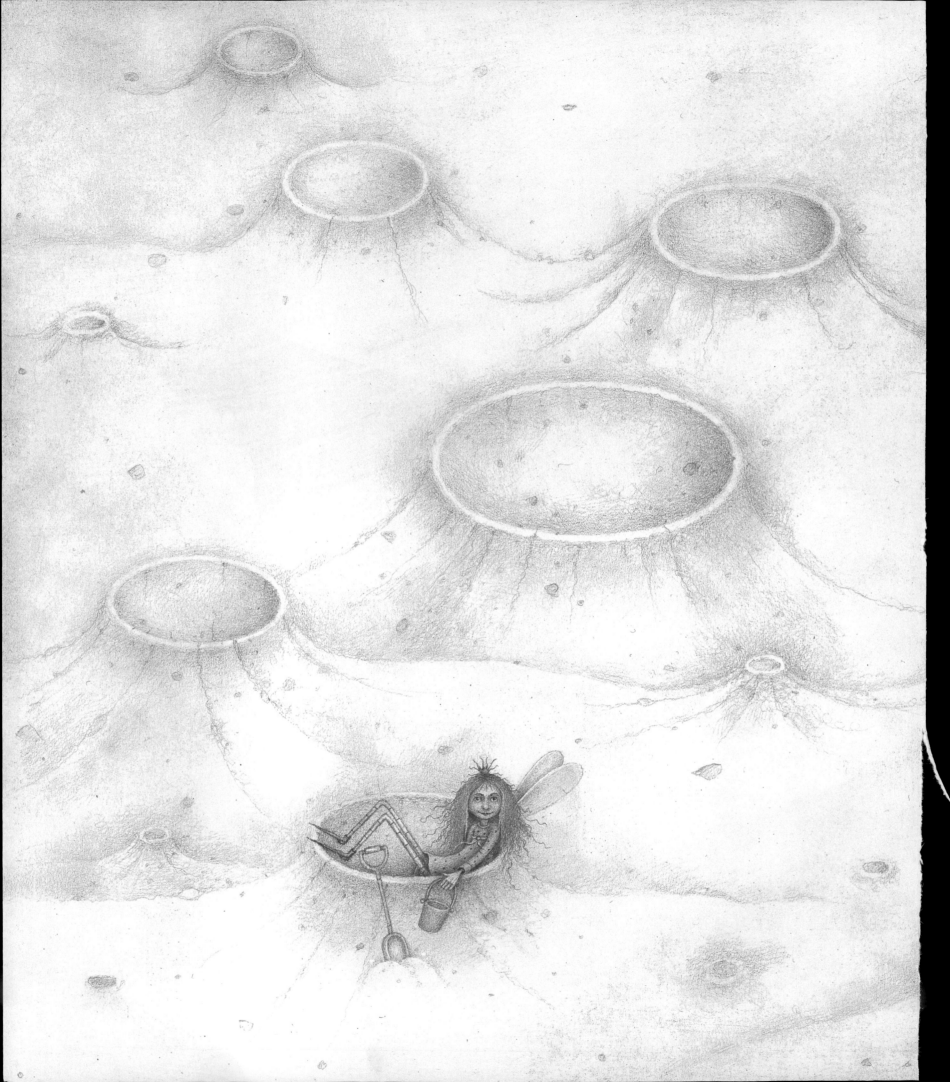